Fragments of my mind

By

Joanna Dinnair

As I type away on this keyboard,

sharing my thoughts openly and deeply to a flat surface.

I wish we had quills and ink.

Straight from the pen to paper, fresh with ink blots and smudges.

Rough around the edges and still alive! That thought captured forever, a snapshot in time.

Like we did for all those yesterdays.

Permanent not airbrushed, edited or deleted away.

So here are some things I have to say....

Fragments, little pieces,

Scraps of memories

That spring forward just for a
moment.

Grab hold of them while you can.

As they scatter like dandelion seeds

And then are gone......

They have been nestling in dark
attic rooms

Waiting to be discovered again

They have been underneath and

In-between

For many years unseen.

A crown of thorns placed upon your head

One that turns to gold when you are dead

It's your turn to suffer in dread

For the ones that twist and cheat instead.

Invisible is pain

The stress the strain

The sorrow

Only carves onto the brow

A deep permanent furrow

As I am weak

The last link in the chain

You will not see tomorrow

I can't do this again.

A talent is a gift, a tool

But if given to a fool

It will decay and waste away

They jest, tease and play

Not realising the treasure they hold

They wear it out 'til it is old.

And they say one day that all the
angels will come down to play.

To share the dance and save us all

But will we be worthy in time?

Please take heed of this rhyme.

Fallen angel

Looks up at the sky,

to ask the reason why?

He has been sent down here to die.

His wings removed he cannot fly

The tears of man he has to cry.

Dreams tell you what you are too
scared to say.

What you want to hide away.

Let them teach you every day.

It's a wicked game they play.

Stuck in a rut

It holds you back

being a painted man.

It's all they see.

They do not take you seriously.

Just look under the skin

at what lies within

Your understanding should then begin.

He is just the same as me

Words can cut deeper than a knife

Words once set free cannot be called back home.

Words can be mean nothing or everything.

Words are the footprints we leave behind.

Please use them well and be kind.

When you talk you cannot listen.

You look but do you actually see.

Noise masks what you don't want to hear.

But in my memory it's oh so clear.

Age makes you see more clearly,

As so much has passed before your eyes.

Or does it make you blind?

As you shut so much out from your mind.

So conditioned to hold things deep inside.

The truth from the young you should not hide.

It's your responsibility

to own your mistakes with pride.

Replace a ghost with a shadow.

So when the sun sets it is gone.

It can haunt you no more.

You can't see his reflection in the
window,

or hear the foot steps behind the door.

Beware the sun will rise again and he is
right back where he was before.

Acceptance just like forgiveness,

If you ask you won't get it.

You must help yourself.

It takes courage to grab it.

Take control,

it will make you strong and whole.

I can see it in your eyes and
the way you smile.

I haven't felt like this in a
while.

I open up,

I let you in.

Let's watch another circus
begin.

And when the show is over,

And the curtain comes down.

I remember I bought the ticket
to see the clown.

And the list goes on,

like a never ending staircase,

step by step by step….

A treadmill of short comings

trip over some,

kick away others,

until the past crumbles away beneath,

and what is chasing you is smothered.

The mind's eye blind,

Tired, busy and bored

Many thoughts grinding against each other

Fighting for attention like a spoilt child

The angriest not the sweetest appear

And the subtleties do not survive.

Windows to the past and a glimpse to a possible future

Giving pictures to a blind man is cruel

Tho he can see more than we

And hears everything so clear.

You take for granted those who
cannot talk back.

Those who are loyal at your feet.

They were here a long time before.

They humour you, and watch as
you stumble and crack.

They pick you up then,

Let you make your mistakes again

But unlike them you never learn.

Imagine a silence,

your heart beat the only sound.

Not even birds singing in the trees

Nothing speaking to your soul

Nothing to make everything ok

That's why every moment you
should cease.

As it passes by in the breeze

Bottle it up, put it away

To open up and remember

One cold dark day.

The morning is crisp and bright
as we watch happiness destroying its
self,
gruesome, cruel and raw.
It almost looks like dancing,
claws entangled.
Intense, unbounded, frightening.
What disturbed the order of nature
to see perfection lose all control and
reason.
What sign to man is this?
Is it a glitch, an error,
genetic deformity?
Indeed it is through young eyes,
but through mine a pure cold terror
ensues
now i long for another morning...

Mentor

Once more you outshine those around you.
A unique light I am eternally drawn to.
Could anything be more secure and complete to
me?
A never ending continuous line, my basis
beneath me, always consistent.
No matter how far away from the central point
never straying.
The closer the more pure and divine it becomes.
I don't want to touch you, I don't need to.
As you are within the very essence of me
secured by ornaments of mine.
The obsessive need to be at one with you for me
to create, to thrive.
This has to be for a reason
I have to give back what has been given.
Literally my life.
Without request though a small token
I give you all that I am.

calm, considered, silent
still you sit to humour your elder
your tutor albeit your inferior
yet with grace speak chosen words
female masks hide perfection
eyelashes flutter a concerto
face lit by shadows of young death
empty years have passed
no delectation to be found
only pulsating walls
visions of lost sentiments
heart still in stasis
another lover relinquished
new suitor to be your muse and saviour
irony to refresh the monotony of creation
suffering no relief from its completion
unfulfilled until this new refrain begins.

Spirited with fire
flourishing over green sea
here labour at depths under me
smashed chairs and dreams
a comical yet inevitable union
you turn to me
my hand cannot reach far enough
it touches unable to grasp
my heart so strong yet not wide enough
to prevent or soften the plunge
the horror of violated innocence
different lands they fight the poison
with crowds of adoration
unfair reward for your pure genius
now I see you, watch your utter splendour,
I beg you stand over me
as I need to breathe.

now i run away from you
safe, for how long? don't follow me
through trees , it dark ,so tired I crawl
not beaten yet , daren't stop 'til dawn

your pack will hunt me down
a presence behind is chasing me
wolves suddenly all around
they pin me to the ground

 heavy breath into my ear
your voice is all i hear

the power of your controlling mind
they do your will, you refuse mine
set me free, I'm no use to you
you wont win, I'm used, rung dry

piercing eyes , I can't breathe
fangs sink in, tear flesh from me
slobbering, scratching ,mauling
I beg and weep and bleed
no escape from you here
as I die I have no fear.

Sickness ensues and I suffer pity,
sympathy does not rest easy.
As dunce is a mask I portray.
Evasive, transparent, defensive.
Switch, twist and rebuke upon my sanctity.
Doubt, confusion, a face I no longer fathom.
Do I wait for the vehemence or cease?
Fortitude a true friend despite the repercussions
like preventing petals being plucked from a
flower.
At risk of fury destroying your wings.
Defiant I respond to the shake of your head,
My solicitous heart in petrified coma.
Created convenience is the armoured path I
follow
Bottled silence, corked hysteria, robotic routine.
Formed at your expense and degradation
Mine and only mine is the valve of release
Steadfast pendulum swings to my tune,
and I announce it from the roof tops!

I stare at you through my cracked veil
from within the reverse of a mirror,
from living you , breathing you , shaping you
to now be separated by the chasm of oblivion.
Your eyes are dark glass,
flitting, drifting, mind twitching,
as you attacked wounded and mutilated me
my heart laid open.
Beautiful exterior of terror ,anxiety
shun a fragile and berserk mind.
The world a bizarre stranger to you
reality a constraint ,a confusing inconvenience.
An alien heart pumping like a startled stag.
I reject you for my own sake.
Tho I want to savour every moment
so many lost , stress clouded kisses.
tho you are separate entity to me.
Tired I beg and weep for exoneration,
pity me not my lethargic neglect.
A conscious decision of surrender
that I will regret this irreparable damage.
I am my own judge to repent to.
Like clay in my hands you become
only what i mould.
Manipulated I am forever putty in yours.

Stupid, naive am I
to question your intentions
try to translate and decipher
cryptic supermarket conations
like dust brushed from a jacket sleeve
my life powders to the floor
dismissed like junk mail
shoved through a narrow closed door
from tiniest murmur of mine
volcanic rumbles shatter
seer through ice glass
neither revere nor matter
your axe slices into me
one piece of meat for your pleasure
pounded, minced , squeezed into bag
sealed and packaged to consume at leisure
frozen solid but inside still raw
but your truth not poised to me to thaw
but a meaning to confusion such as this
surely, simply a kiss...............?

cupid continues to fly on broken wings
how many have shot him down
with sharpened arrows of deep despair
I have more putrid blackened wounds than he
yet still I fling myself in front of blunted spears
to fill a gapping hungry void, I try to engulf them
at speed they glance through me with no pain
as immune to it am I
I still yearn, crave, breathe it
nothing will ever rock deep enough to
satisfy my appetite for a sublime symbiosis
an empty shell fed only on crumbs of bread
within my mind
I slug through a deep marsh up to my knees,
capable mud drags at my feet
tips of green reeds struggle yet resolve to poke
through like hope......
I glance up at the opulent clouds
a golden speck, fresh cherub cheeks now glide
and i sigh, sink, sucked down, complete.

Protect me , throw criminals to the deck
see me strong in my throne of power.
Persuade me , seduce me, lure me
tho i was entangled in another
but alas!
I succumbed.
are my clothes a mask?
swathed from head to toe.
A trial you take upon yourself
tho incompatible are we
you wash me, feed me , secure me
scrape me up off the floor
along with remnants of my face
my life, my very soul
insides now dead, eroding
I cannot harbour life
two rejected spawn from sterile loins
lie begging in the gutter.

Standing under the street lamp
in the bitter cold rain
pitied and rejected
see the sorry state before you
I am weak behind my jeers
Hysterical I have been released at last.
Still you climb onto my flailing shoulders
to carry for you eternity
you give my punishment as this burden
because without you to love
I am just empty
I owe you this much.

a blindness
we thought we saw kindness
just a clever rehearsed mask
opaque to you and me.

Contain small implants of pain
dart itinerate back and forth, as
ardent verbal intercourse becomes carnal.
laid bare deepest sorrows, warped nurture
in severable interest, duplicate icons,
we twain custodians manoeuvre ever forward
brains racing, bodies flagging, spirit exalted
fake form and past shadows over us
preventing us, restraining us, determined
bow down to inner fortitude
embrace , stave and regard
renounce my psyche, endure , regain purpose
in perpetuity ,indebted and appeased
strive to nullify small implants of pain
yesterday dies tomorrow surely survives.

Pictures flashing by
I contemplate my future
from whence i came to where i reside
still inside , inertia jerks
what is this journey?
all be it inevitable
bold coloured lines , no cheer, sheer drudgery
faceless bodies withdraw and shut down
warm inside, stuffed into the corner
await freezing white light
what has changed in me through this passage
am I the same?
one woman in , another out
each side a different lifetime, a choice
but which to choose
which is real , which is me, which is sane
maybe I don't want to rest
forever split
an unstable nucleus remains within
my pale now silent guise.

after a long journey into the arms of consistency
where tenderness has an original unaltered state
of self
as in the beginning, no pretence,
nothing alluding to the suggestions of age
or the masks of adversity,
the challenges of monotony
a texture of divinity, purity and potential
makes time forever still and conquered
then cleansed to embark onwards,
the shackles of subservience, unbound, release me
enlightened by a revelation that I am,
no longer sneered at like dirt on a shoe or,
flushed out like hair in a plug hole
but revered for what is sacred,
piece by piece such foundations can only bind
with the solid mortar of kisses from gilded angels
a life of beaming smiles,
creation of works
the substance of love.

With incomprehensible strength of mind i pity....
that Rome was not built in a day
for my new world was forged in an instant
from the innocence, respect and devotion
in the furnace of your eyes.....
this intensity I bottle and pour into my empty heart,
absorbed,
harnessing an energy akin only the first breath of
 a new born child
with no fear just electricity
I sacrifice myself to you my creator,
I am born again.

as i sit,
a sideways glance through the window
partial reflection of light
and my reticence bounce back
altered, disjointed , angled
on the other side of the "pain" of glass
people, hunched shoulders, furrowed brows
seem deeper than my own
this astounds me
does this shard protect me?
or am I mirroring my own ignorance
on which side do I sit or hide?
vacant faces run past in the rain
glance in, see me illuminated in ardour
to them I epitomise sanctuary
to me...... relief
i am not under their cloud.

As I stand between blue parallel lines
in an almost grey darkness - i wonder
what will plug the hole in this emptiness?
the hole that sucks the hope though it,
i know what radiates on the other side
an excitement lingers ,
desperate inside me
sick of waiting at a bus stop
to which the routes have changed
wishing for the express...
i know he is not my destination.

To be content, my heart is a jigsaw
made up of love to and from different sources.
though there are still spaces
he does not seem to fit
and he is not the intrinsic part
to hold it all together
a temporary stop gap 'tis all
this puzzle will never be complete
but gradually filled with gems,
and removing disguised imposters
through the journey of my life
yet no one has pieces enough
to end the quest for the stable four corners
is the final piece simply hidden within my mind?
locked away by a fear of conformity
a secret hope that there is a higher plain than this
and I will find a mate to exalt my soul
to stop searching is to admit heaven does not exist
so one carries on eternally in limbo
thriving off snatched sparks in the air
oh how they charge me!
balancing with an on/off current i rest easy
battery of my heart never to be flat
whilst my mind still beats.

Too tired to sleep,
so an artificial consciousness begins.
in all innocence i return, defences baited
my heart strings so long, are knotted and
tangled
dreams dragged out by the roots like weeds
no knights to joust in my honour,
all shields dented
you can see right into me, through me, past
me
why can't I see into your eyes,
such a thick veil
like ice with transparent skin,
pin pricked veins pierce
 my skull a mountain range,
face a patchwork
trembling hands with articulated fingers
ivy and thorns grow through your rib cage
my spine twisted in torment.

Stomach bloated, strangled
only selective hearing, erased memories,
created conversations
a mime of life , a dance of ideals
a theatre of warped minds stage elusive games
a charade I do not wish to act in,
I breathe, it's so unsettling
our cogs do not align,
They are cut from clashing stone
your turbines chip away as mine crumble and
erode
emerge not polished , pristine , iridescent
but a tarnished, muted , like a dowdy foul, my
body on a platter.
My mind carved, wings sliced
I'm trimmed with garnish and stuffed with
pleasantries
prize bird silenced, dine on me
As I calmly say what I am
"for display purposed only"

Crab apples all fall at the same time each year,
who flicks the switch?
this un-comprehended, gets trampled upon
merely soiling shoes!
an unfinished black and white sketch
areas of shading with detail missing.
giant hamster wheel goes round and around
tourist gabble , entertained?
programmed to want nothing better
dust spills up as an old trainer kicks the gravel
somehow over tuned in, saturated with colour
over exposed , obliterated with information
hand held drones in concrete hives
fashion puppets on a string, no plastic, no beauty
money flows through veins furred with prejudice
forced abuse by cholesterol, to gorge buys silence
opticians diagnose greed, reputation blinds,
minds destroyed in aluminium boxes,
misshapen locks
different weaknesses with a different key
monkey why did this one fit?

Flash , brazen , dressed in ill-fitting white.
Adorned with jewellery as fake as your smile.
gangster who seduced yourself an empire.
village in your pocket lined too deep
looming and drinking ,
teary eyed drama queen
in more ways than one it transpires to black
and blue
bruised from silent enemy,
concealed by drunken mishap
love is not enough
if donated by a struggling pauper

She runs through endless fields,
Concrete fields of steel
With too much space to breathe
within the ashes still lie the deplorable iniquity
of a mother hypnotised by power and the pound
sign
The pressure of the everyday monotonies of
life,
Time is wasted, it moves so fast
the world a big worrying mess.
over coffee I ponder are there any positives.
Just nature? air?
That's what I need!
I shall suffocate no more!

A MOMENT WITH A KING

I tread the leaves where she herself once walked.
I know it is dusk, but through the trees I see
time rewind silently. I look down and see a
locket entwined in the bracken. A tiny pewter
book with four pages. "The past, the present, the
future and the spaces in between" is scratched
into the metal. As I grasp it, I feel the pumping
of a weak blood line travel up through my
third finger, too deep within me. Time behind
the trees stops. I carry on down the path,
familiar yet with pieces missing. Ahead a
fountain, within its spray a full and beautiful
spectrum. I thought for a moment I hear a child
whisper. There she sits on a bench behind the
fountain, beckoning me closer. I am not
afraid, I feel solid, drawn to the soil. My roots
are here. I arrive, look down upon her. She
scolds me for being late. We turn left and
stroll to a manor. Through a gateway, then
studded door .Down dark oak clad halls to
where he sits in all his splendour. Now this,
THIS is more than a walk in the park! As I

kneel before his majesty I feel a glory, a power, a strength and beauty no text book or tour guided trip can convey. A deep bellowing tone, black eyes sparkle.

"I have one thing to say before I send you on your way as I can all but bare the stench of despair. I vibrate in my grave at what you in your epoch have become. You say you are now civilised, yet even with the inventions and knowledge to create, preserve and prolong life, you destroy the very earth you walk upon. Yes I was a barbarian, with no moral fortitude, but an honest proud grafting people were we, not leeches on the hands that fed us! Who won you your freedom? I pity you as I watch you weighed down by tiny inconveniences and disgusted as you walk by the ooh so many collection tins. If you learn one thing today. Look at the innocence and fair view of a child, preserve that in each and every one of you and in turn you preserve your survival. I shall leave now hoping the modern educated, civilised and mechanical man still has a conscience not to live just for the moment. That he learns from

his roots and his foundations to preserve what
gave him life and to give it back tenfold"
I crumble to the floor, all our shame weighs
heavy upon me. He roars. "Pick yourself up! I
should trample you under my foot, but for the
natural order of things I give you that life is
an eternal cycle. The past the present, the
future and us living in the spaces between. I
tell you this to save myself and all of us.
We are all the same just repeating the
same mistakes in a different time. I only state
the obvious. Go back down your path with my
sight in your eyes. Then I shall no longer pity
and carry disappointment for dystopian
man."
The locket drops from my hand, time fast
forwards and now I'm walking back home.
Then there tattooed on my flesh are the words
spaces in-between.
We shall live them, fill them, change them
rejoice in them and now heal them.......

Beauty is fragile
Those with it don't know its power
Like a rose has a thorn
It lures you in this subtle flower

Heart broken by one so young
Love covered my eyes
Deaf dumb and blind
Would never have dreamed that you lied
What should I have done?

Time slows down
When you're waiting in line
Then speeds right up
When you feel just fine
It's so precious
Don't waste mine

There is nothing so empty than a blank
page
Nothing with so much potential, clean
and inviting
With endless possibilities of greatness
It stares back at me, it overwhelms me
I could give it everything,
And still have nothing left
And still it begs for more,
I can't give it what it deserves

Walls close in
Stumbling blind
I pray I can find a better sin
Taste the bitter
The sweet I cannot find

You had everything I wanted
I could have taken everything you had
But I held myself back
My broken heart has never hurt so bad.
But I loved him enough to let him go
And I had not earned the right
To make you sad, so I said no.

The heart pulled in opposite directions
Can only cause it to break
The shock waves
Are more than we can take.
So be faithful
For god's sake.

Most people need it though it's killing me
It fortifies most but consumes me
It is invisible inside me
If you want to help me bleed me

It wells up
I beat it down
It still rears its ugly head
My soul turns against me
And I'm filled with dread

Time - the one thing you can never get
enough of or replace
It never stands still
Use it up because you can't tie it down
Stand and look it square in the face.

I can see the temperature of your heart
Passionate and fiery hot
Through my dead eyes
You can see mine is ice cold
I take your anger as an attack
As I have no idea what I've got.

You left me outside in the pouring rain
I never want to feel that way again
Having to be fed and bathed
In so much pain
By a hero who had his own stress and
strain
I thank you
I don't know where to start.

A baby cries
Swept aside
By who had her inside
Love and life denied.

Loss is tough
Loss is empty
Loss is rough
Loss can get harder every day
Loss gives you the chance to say
I love you now you have been taken
away.

Man in a hat
Struts his stuff
He screams
"It's never enough!"
But he works so hard
And he is tough
And he will prove
He has grown up.

Graffiti drips from the walls, it is part of our landscape. Our eyes are closed so we do not see the stains. So we are numb, there is no impact, no disgust, no eyelids battered. No need to wash it clean. There is paper over the cracks. We absorb the grey silence. Deaf to the undecipherable wall of noise. Bright yet artificial is the light. People forced shoulder to shoulder yet each one alone. Snide plump chickens take the grain oh so freely scattered to them. Fine thin elegant peacocks scratch about for unwanted scraps.

Their feathers torn asunder to pay for it all. For how long can nature resist and tip the balance once more.

Black is made of all colours
Slack is the eye and the mind
Back to the eyes of a child
Crack open to see what you'll find

Expectation
the pressure to live up to
Your Anticipation
Of what you want me to do
My desperation
that how you feel is untrue.

And now all I see is red
My heart feels like lead
From how I felt before
Those rose tinted glasses
are here no more.

Don't suffocate the music
Don't stifle our dreams
Don't trample on opinions
Don't choke our voices
Don't shake that can!
Coz you know what will happen...

Without what you lost
where would you be now
despite what it cost.....

Laser is the rain
cuts right through the pain
I walk through it once again
It helps me to release the strain.

Do I walk in their shoes
as I dance to the beat of their drum
I don't sing my own tune
Embarrassed of what I've become
Do I choose my own way
Still do what they say
Or just take a chance everyday.

Blankets cover
Or they can smother
Beware the devil
Who cares for his brother
From his lies
The truth we can discover.

And so I sit and wait
And so I sit and stare
As life it passes by
It doesn't even wave
Or say goodbye.

And so it begins
The endless run of things
I thought it would be bliss
but it's the chaos that I miss
the chaos is outside
And all we can do is hide
Until we are free once more
I can't wait for the madness I adore.

Robots with human eyes
It won't be long until they fool us
with their disguise.
Will we notice?
Will we realise?
Get ready to say your goodbyes.

Worn down fingers
Hunched shoulders
Eyes are bleeding
Please don't tell me
We are succeeding
Please go backwards
I wake up screaming
Please tell me
I have been dreaming!

So what is real?
Is what I see just what I feel
What I want the world to be
I've got a feeling I am not free...

Surrender is not comfortable
A concept as alien as me
If I am yours
Then what am I going to be
A construct
Just what you want to see

Is it safer to be alone?
No hurt
No pain
No one to blame?

I wish I could open a door
And through my mind
give you a tour
I'm sure would find it such a bore
My aching heart is so sore
All I want is for you to adore
These crazy hopes and dreams
For us together to explore.

LIFE IS A
SEE-SAW

GET THE BALANCE
RIGHT

The love of a creature
Pure, untainted, unconditional
As nature is wise
It has learnt its lessons
It does not need to question
Or push against reason
We bang our heads against invisible
brick walls
we have built for ourselves
That will never come down
As the earth laughs
And let us make our mistakes.

Instant tension
Hackles up!
Like a bolt of electricity
I flee
Drawn to the fresh air
Like it's a drug
My instincts tell me it's not to be.

Selfishness is the cure
I was blind to the obvious
when others took what they wanted
for themselves.
They swallowed me up
And played with me like a toy
No part of this did I enjoy
I am better off by myself.

Down dark alley ways
I look into the puddles on the street
How many souls have passed
beneath my feet.
I wish the reflections could speak.

I came from far away
and I am here to stay
As I am now in your bones
And in your soul
Even your mind I can control
You never need
to live without me at all.

My life
Just like a coffee stain
Leaves a mark
But is soon wiped away

Love is not possession
But you know that on you I depend
As my joints they do not bend
And my mind cannot retrieve
The words to beg
Can you please leave.

Tough love
Is hard to give
It's the job I have been given
To teach you how to live.

We live in artificial confusion
To keep us at bay
It's all an illusion
And one day
I hope and I pray
That the blinkers will be removed
And we will all say
We are free and so
We forgive the intrusion.

This is a collection of my poetry some of which has been available to read before on Instagram or Writer's Cafe

I wanted to bring it together to raise awareness for people suffering from Haemochromatosis who suffer so many different symptoms silently every day as Iron builds up and damages their bodies.
Please support the charity if you can.

The Haemochromatosis Society

Thank you for reading some of the fragments
of my mind.
Joanna Dinnair 2021

Keep in touch with my work on Instagram

@dinnair poetry

So now you show an interest
when its all said and done.

Jealous of what I have become.

You had the chance to become one.

Now it's broken, now its numb.

I cover my eyes

I block my ears

I free my mind

From all my fears

I shut the door

I lock the gate

I close the door and

Wipe away the tears.

It feels like it is just beginning

although it is near the end.

No tears were ever shed

It doesn't matter that my mind was fed

with Empty promises.

I had everything I wanted.

And believed every word you said.

I wish we would not
Put a bird in a cage
Take a fish from water
Cut a rose from its stem
Or send a lamb to the slaughter

Reassurance is all I need
On it my love will feed
And blossom at your touch
Just your presence is not enough
As your mind drifts away
Leave your heart with me to stay
Even if it is just for today.

Always searching
But never finding
Anything at all
Because it's already here
Waiting for you
It was right under your nose
After all.

Check out Cheap Accessory by
Self Isolation Network
A project I had the pleasure to write the
lyrics for.
Available from Bandcamp
Cheap Accessory | Self Isolation Network (bandcamp.com)

A novella, the first in the series of the relationship between Georgia and Brodie. Where murder and heartbreak are at every turn.
Part 2 Professional Groupie coming soon…

Printed in Great Britain
by Amazon

59803320R00039

words are the
foot prints we
leave behind....

A collection of
poetry written
over the last ten
years by Joanna
Dinnair from
London

ISBN 9798713444327

90000

9 798713 444327

Pike's Quest

Don't forget to moisturise!

K J Bennett